Kimmie Koala and Friends
Short Stories, Fuzzy Animals, and Life Lessons

Karma for Kids Books

Norma MacDonald

Kimmie Koala and Friends
Short Stories, Fuzzy Animals, and Life Lessons

Copyright © 2016 Norma Macdonald

First Edition

Published by: Find Your Way Publishing, Inc.
PO BOX 667
Norway, ME 04268 U.S.A.
www.findyourwaypublishing.com

ISBN-13: 978-1-945290-03-9

ISBN-10: 1-945290-03-X

Library of Congress Control Number: 2016940927

Printed in the United States of America.

Dedication

This book is dedicated to all of the people trying to make the world a better place. You are making a positive difference!

""Doing good holds the power to transform us on the inside, and then ripple out in ever-expanding circles that positively impact the world at large." ~ Shari Arison

Table of Contents

About This Book

Welcome to our Karma for Kids Books Series. We are very grateful that you picked up this book. We believe together we can make a positive difference, one child at a time. We strive to instill important life lessons in the lives of young children. We are firm believers in Karma and think that if this simple Law of the Universe is taught to children at a young age, their lives will have the potential to be absolutely amazing.

We once knew a dog named Karma. She was a beautiful, yellow Labrador retriever. It wasn't until after she passed, at 11 years old (God bless her loyal soul.), that we realized just how fitting her name really was.

Karma is indeed a retriever.

Whatever we threw out, Karma was always happy to bring it back to us. It didn't matter what it was, she always brought it back. If we threw out garbage, she'd bring it back without question. If we threw out the most beautiful dog toy, she'd bring it back. It's the same in life. Whatever you send out, is what you will get back. Guaranteed. Every time. Our Karma for Kids Book Series hopes to instill this easy-to-understand Law of the Universe into the lives of children at a young age. The Universe wants to happily bring you all that your heart desires, and it will, effortlessly. But first, you've got to throw out what you want it to bring back to you so that it can! Have fun with this and watch the magic happen. God bless!

Find all of Norma MacDonald's Karma for Kids Books at Amazon.com.

For more of our Karma for Kids books please visit us at:

www.karmaforkidsbooks.wordpress.com
or
www.findyourwaypublishing.com

Other books that we recommend to help children learn important life lessons:

The Many Adventures of Peppy the Emperor Penguin: Short Stories, Fuzzy Animals, and Life Lessons by Norma MacDonald

Lucy Llama and Friends: Short Stories, Fuzzy Animals, and Life Lessons by Norma MacDonald

Ethan Eagle and Friends: Short Stories, Fuzzy Animals, and Life Lessons by Norma MacDonald

Billy Brown Bear and Friends: Short Stories, Fuzzy Animals, and Life Lessons by Norma MacDonald

Humble Heron and Friends: Short Stories, Fuzzy Animals, and Life Lessons by Norma MacDonald

Peter Penguin and Friends: Short Stories, Fuzzy Animals and Life Lessons by Norma MacDonald

Guaranteed Success for Kindergarten; 50 Easy Things You Can Do Today! by Marrae Kimball

Guaranteed Success for Grade School; 50 Easy Things You Can Do Today! by Marrae Kimball

The Secret Combination to Middle School: Real Advice from Real Kids, Ideas for Success, and Much More! by Marrae Kimball

Thank you!

Kimmie Koala and Friends

Short Stories, Fuzzy Animals, and Life Lessons

Karma for Kids Books

Norma MacDonald

Chapter One

You Earned It

THE SCHOOL YEAR WAS coming to an end and all of the students in Mr. Ostrich's class were extremely excited for summer vacation to start. Shawna Sheep had plans to go to the pool every day so she could swim. Kimmie Koala had plans to go away to summer camp. Joey Jaguar had plans to read as many books as he could. Zach Zebra had plans to play with his friends whenever he could.

Everyone was looking forward to sunny days with no school or homework or class or boring Mr. Ostrich blabbing on and on about the lesson of the day. Just two more weeks of school and they were free!

"Class, this year we are going to have a final exam to assess everything you learned in the past few months. It will cover vocabulary, science, and mathematics," Mr. Ostrich announced.

The class moaned and groaned. Everyone was already in summer mode and the thought of having to study for one last test was too much.

When class was dismissed the four friends went outside to the playground to wait for their parents to pick them up.

"I can't believe we have to study for one more test!" Shawna Sheep whined.

"I can barely even focus on my homework anymore!" Joey Jaguar complained.

"Well we already learned all those things, so it won't be that bad," said Kimmie Koala.

Zach Zebra nodded and said, "We will barely even have to study because we already learned all of the stuff that will be on the test."

Shawna Sheep was picked up first and she decided not to tell her parents about the test. If they knew about it, they wouldn't let her play outside until she studied, and the sun was shining too bright to stay inside. When she got home she tossed her books onto her bed and ran outside and played until the sun went down.

Joey Jaguar was picked up next. He told his parents that he just needed to get together all of his vocabulary words from the year. Once he gathered all of the lists, he tucked them away into the folder.

"That's enough studying for this test," he thought, and then he went outside to play.

Kimmie Koala went home that night and told her parents about the test. She gathered all of her notes and homework assignments and organized them by subject. Then she made flashcards to study and asked her parents to quiz her on the information.

Zach Zebra told his parents about the test but decided that he didn't want to start studying yet. He felt confident that he knew most of what he needed to and that he could review it all the next day.

The next day in class Mr. Ostrich passed out a practice test. To no one's surprise, Kimmie Koala got an A.

"How did you remember all of that stuff?" Joey Jaguar asked.

"I studied a lot last night to practice," Kimmie Koala said.

Shawna Sheep scoffed. "I didn't study at all. It was too nice outside yesterday to stay in and do homework. This practice test was enough, now I remember everything."

Joey Jaguar and Zach Zebra agreed with Shawna Sheep.

That night when all the friends went home Kimmie Koala was the only one who did more studying. Shawna Sheep, Zach Zebra, and Joey Jaguar all met up at the park to play basketball.

"I can't believe Kimmie Koala is missing this!" Zach Zebra said.

"She will regret it when we all get A's and she realizes she didn't have to do so much studying," said Shawna Sheep.

Joey Jaguar wanted to keep playing, but he thought that maybe Kimmie Koala was onto something. "Maybe she is right, guys, I think I'm going to go home and study a little bit."

For the next few nights leading up to the test, Kimmie Koala spent all of her time studying. She wanted to get 100%. Shawna Sheep and Zach Zebra continued to play outside after school. Joey Jaguar played with them after school but when he went home for dinner, he studied a little bit.

Finally, it was the day of the test.

Mr. Ostrich stood up in front of the class holding the stack of papers up for everyone to see. He said, "The test will take you until the lunch bell. If you finish early just bring it up to my desk and you can have an early recess."

The test was passed out and everyone picked up their pencils and started scribbling answers onto the blank lines.

Shawna Sheep was excited about the possibility of an early recess so she rushed through the test. If she didn't know an answer she just guessed. She didn't study anyway, so she didn't really care.

Joey Jaguar got stumped on the very first question. It was a math problem, his weakest subject. He started to worry that maybe not studying wasn't the best idea. He did his best and answered the questions to the best of his ability but eventually he got so frustrated that he just guessed on the whole second half of the test and then joined Shawna Sheep on the playground.

Zach Zebra knew most of the answers, but there were some that he was unsure of. Maybe if he had spent more time studying he would have a better chance at figuring the answers out.

Kimmie Koala was having no problem at all. She read each question carefully and wrote out her work neatly to ensure that Mr. Ostrich would be able to read it. When she completed every question she went back to the beginning to check it over. All of the studying she did after school really paid off, she felt like she had the correct answer for everything. She handed her test in when the lunch bell rang.

"That was easy!" Kimmie Koala said at the lunch table. "How do you think you all did?"

Zach Zebra shrugged. "I think I knew most of the answers, but there were a few that I never got around to studying. I probably got a B, but hopefully, I can pull off an A!"

Joey Jaguar frowned. "I probably should have spent some time studying, but I definitely knew some of them. The math questions were hard and I had to guess on a lot of them."

Shawna Sheep stayed quiet until everyone looked at her. She said, "I had to guess on a few, but I knew most of them. It's all stuff we learned before, that's why I didn't study. I bet I will at least get a B." Unfortunately, Shawna Sheep did not believe herself. She knew that she probably failed the test.

After school, all four friends were finally free to play together. They played hide and seek in the park until sundown then they all went home for supper.

Shawna Sheep had trouble falling asleep. She was so worried that failing the test would hold her back and all of her friends would go to the next grade without her. "Mr. Ostrich wouldn't do that to me. He would never give me an F," she thought. The thought comforted her and she was finally able to doze off into a sleep.

The next day in class Mr. Ostrich had all of the tests graded and ready to hand back. "We had one perfect score," he said, "so a big congratulation to Kimmie Koala!" He handed her the test with a big red 100 in a circle.

He continued to hand out the tests. Zach Zebra got a B and he was happy that had made some time to study because it paid off. Joey Jaguar got a C and he was sad that it wasn't a good grade, but he knew that he should have studied more.

Shawna Sheep saw the grade on Joey Jaguar's test and knew that she would probably get the same one since they two of them played together every night and didn't do any studying. But when Mr. Ostrich handed Shawna Sheep her graded test there was a big red F on it. Her heart sank.

When the lunch bell rang the whole entire class ran to the cafeteria, but Shawna Sheep stayed behind. Once the classroom was empty, she marched right up to Mr. Ostrich's desk and put the test down.

"Mr. Ostrich, why did you give me an F? I've been a good student all year. I don't think I deserve an F."

"Well Shawna Sheep, you got an F because most of your answers on the test were wrong. I didn't give you an F, you earned an F."

"But I have received good grades all year!"

"Let me ask you something," said Mr. Ostrich, "Did you study for this test?"

Shawna Sheep blushed. "No."

"You see Shawna Sheep, the work you put into something, and the amount of time you put into something, well it will show in the end result. Since you did not study for this test, it is showing in your poor grade. You received good grades all year because you worked hard, right?"

Shawna Sheep nodded. She realized that just because she learned things during the year, it didn't mean she could be lazy when it came time for a test. She knew that from now on she would work hard on all of her assignments, and study for her tests, to make sure the end result was always something she would be proud of.

"Mr. Ostrich, I've learned my lesson, and I will not let this happen again. Can I please have some extra credit homework, or retake the test, to try to bring my grade up?"

"I'm glad that you learned from this," said Mr. Ostrich, "I will see what I can come up with and get back to you."

Shawna Sheep went home somewhat relieved and was looking forward to doing better next time.

Chapter Two

Jump

DURING SUMMER VACATION, Shawna Sheep spend her days at the community swimming pool. She invited her friends to join her whenever they were free. One day, all four friends were playing in the pool, splashing each other, playing Marco Polo, and practicing their dives from the edge of the pool.

"Who wants to go with me to jump off the high dive?" Kimmie Koala asked the group.

"'I will!" Zach Zebra shouted out.

The two of them hopped out of the pool and ran over to the diving pool. There were three diving boards: the low one, the medium one, and the high one. Kimmie Koala loved adventures and challenges so whenever she was at the pool she wanted to jump off the high dive as many times as possible.

For Shawna Sheep, she spent so much time at the pool that the high dive wasn't that exciting anymore. She did it once and that was enough, it wasn't worth waiting in line anymore.

Zach Zebra had never jumped from the high dive before so he was really excited to give it a try. His stomach was tied in a knot and his heart was thumping loudly with excitement and nervousness.

"You don't want to come?" Kimmie Koala asked Shawna Sheep and Joey Jaguar.

"That line is too long, it's not worth it," said Shawna Sheep.

"Yeah, we will just stay here and watch you guys," said Joey Jaguar.

Joey Jaguar felt like his heart was in his throat, that's how hard it was pounding in his chest. His friends didn't know that he was terrified of heights. He was thankful that Shawna Sheep didn't want to wait in line because it gave him a reason to not go off the high dive without telling them he was too scared.

Kimmie Koala and Zach Zebra ran to the line while the lifeguards blew their whistles and yelled at them to walk.

"This is going to be so much fun!" Zach Zebra squealed while he jumped up and down in place.

"It is the best! It's so high up there you feel like you are going to keep falling forever!" Kimmie Koala could barely wait for her turn.

Back in the pool Shawna Sheep and Joey Jaguar watched as their friends got closer and closer to the front of the line.

"It takes so long just to have a few seconds of fun; I don't waste my time like that anymore. Jumping once was enough for me," said Shawna Sheep.

Joey Jaguar didn't say anything. He didn't want anyone to know that he had never jumped from the high dive before.

When it came time for Zach Zebra to climb the ladder all of his friends watched as he pulled himself from one rung to the next until he was standing all the way up on top of the high dive. Just watching his friend climb that high made Joey Jaguar feel uneasy.

"That's really high," he whispered to Shawna Sheep.

"Yeah, but it's still not worth the wait," she said.

Zach Zebra was starting to feel more nervous, but he knew that he had to jump so that Kimmie Koala could go next. He walked slowly to the very end of the diving board and looked down. The water seemed to be miles away. He took a deep breath and then jumped.

All of his friends cheered for him, then it was Kimmie Koala's turn. She scurried up the ladder quickly. When she reached the top she took a running start and jumped right off without hesitation.

"That was awesome!" Zach Zebra said to her once she was back down on the ground with him and they walked back to the pool where their friends were waiting for them.

Zach Zebra and Kimmie Koala both had huge smiles on their faces. They were both filled with adrenaline from jumping off the high dive.

"You guys should have come with us! It was awesome!" Zach Zebra said.

"Oh well, maybe next time," said Joey Jaguar.

"Have you ever jumped before?" Kimmie Koala asked. "I don't think we ever did it together."

"Yeah," said Shawna Sheep, "I don't think I ever saw you jump either."

Joey Jaguar felt his heart start beating even faster and his face was turning red. He didn't want to lie to his friends because he knew it was wrong to lie, but he didn't want them to know about his fear of heights.

"No," he said, "I never jumped from the high dive." He took a deep breath and waited for them to start laughing at him.

"I don't blame you," said Shawna Sheep, "I don't have the patience to wait in line either."

Joey Jaguar felt relieved that they just thought it was because he didn't want to wait in the line. He didn't correct Shawna Sheep and they went back to playing pool games, but Zach Zebra didn't let it go.

"But you have to try it just once!"

"Yeah," said Kimmie Koala, "The line wasn't even really that long. It's worth it!"

"Come on Joey Jaguar. I'll go again with you!" Zach Zebra pulled Joey Jaguar toward the steps of the pool.

"No!" Joey Jaguar screamed so loud that it made everyone stop what they were doing and look over to see what was happening. "Sorry, it's just that I'm pretty scared of heights and the thought of climbing that high and then jumping off doesn't sound very fun to me."

"I was scared too," said Zach Zebra, "but I promise it's really fun. Don't you just want to try it one time?"

"Yeah, I want to try it, but I'm too afraid," said Joey Jaguar.

"We will cheer for you and encourage you," said Kimmie Koala.

"I think you will be glad you tried it," said Shawna Sheep.

"Come on!" said Zach Zebra, "Let's all go to support Joey Jaguar for his first high dive adventure!"

The four friends got out of the pool and headed for the diving pool. Joey Jaguar was getting more and more nervous the closer they got to the high dive line. He was so scared he couldn't even talk!

"Do you want to go first?" Zach Zebra asked.

Joey Jaguar shook his head no.

"Last?" Kimmie Koala asked.

Joey Jaguar shook his head no.

"Second?" Shawna Sheep asked.

Joey Jaguar nodded.

"Okay, well I will go first," said Shawna Sheep, "that way I'm out of this line sooner!"

While Shawna Sheep climbed the ladder, Joey Jaguar watched in horror.

"Are you scared, Joey Jaguar?" asked Kimmie Koala.

Joey Jaguar nodded.

"Don't be scared, it's fun. You will feel so proud of yourself after you conquer your fear!" Kimmie Koala gave Joey Jaguar a pat on the back to comfort him.

Shawna Sheep made it to the top, jumped off, and then swam to the edge. That meant it was Joey Jaguar's turn to make the climb.

"You can do it!" Zach Zebra cheered.

Joey Jaguar climbed up the ladder very slowly. His mind was racing with fear. What if the ladder broke and he fell onto the concrete? What if the pool wasn't deep enough and he smacked the bottom? What if he tripped on the edge of the diving board? What if he forgot how to swim by the time he splashed into the pool? He could only think of the worst possibilities.

When he got to the top he looked down at his friends. They looked so small, just little specks along the floor, the floor he wished he could have his feet on.

"Go Joey Jaguar!" He could hear them cheering. He knew that he had to jump. If he climbed back down he would not only disappoint his friends, but he would also disappoint himself.

He took one step toward the end of the diving board. He felt like he was going to be sick he was so nervous. When he reached the end of the diving board he paused.

Below him, his friends were chanting his name. He knew that they believed in him. "I can do this!" he said to himself. Then he stepped off the diving board. The feeling of falling happened so fast and the next thing he knew; he was in the pool.

When he swam up above the water all of his friends were hooting and hollering and clapping wildly. "You did it!!!"

Joey Jaguar was so proud of himself for going outside of his comfort zone and trying something new. The best part was, his friends were right, jumping off the high dive was a blast! Joey Jaguar decided to make a promise to himself to always try new things, even if he was scared.

Chapter Three

One Is Silver and The Other Is Gold

DURING SUMMER VACATION, a new family moved into the neighborhood. The Bobcat family came from the mountains and moved in right down the street from Kimmie Koala. The new family in town had a daughter the same age as Kimmie Koala and all of her friends.

Becky Bobcat was nervous about being in a new town but was also really excited to make new friends. After she unpacked all of her things into her new room she ran outside to introduce herself to her neighbors.

"Hi!" Becky Bobcat shouted across the lawn to Kimmie Koala. "I'm Becky Bobcat and I just moved to town from the mountains. What is your name?"

Kimmie Koala was surprised that Becky Bobcat wasn't shy at all. If it was Kimmie Koala who was new in town, she would probably have trouble making new friends. She thought it was really cool that Becky Bobcat wasn't shy.

"I'm Kimmie Koala. Do you want to come over and play?" Kimmie Koala decided that she should be nice to Becky Bobcat since she didn't know anyone else in the neighborhood and moved far away from all of her friends.

"Sure!" Becky Bobcat agreed and ran over to play with Kimmie Koala.

The two new friends played with the hose outside, spraying each other with water and laughing. They were running around having the best time. Kimmie Koala was excited to have a new friend. She couldn't wait to introduce Becky Bobcat to all of the other kids, she knew they would love having a new friend too.

"You should come with me to the park tomorrow to play soccer with all of my friends," said Kimmie Koala.

"I would love to!" Becky Bobcat was very happy that she met someone so nice on her first day of living in a new place. "Do you want to come over for dinner tonight?"

"Okay!" said Kimmie Koala, "I just have to go home and ask my mom and dad first." Kimmie Koala ran inside to tell her parents that she had made a new friend and to ask if she could eat dinner there.

"Mom! Dad!" Kimmie Koala yelled. "Can I eat dinner at Becky Bobcats house? She is our new neighbor and my new best friend."

Mrs. Koala came downstairs. "Did you forget that you made plans with Shawna Sheep, Joey Jaguar, and Zach Zebra tonight? I thought I was going to drive you to meet them at the movie theater."

"Oh yeah…"

"Why don't you invite Becky Bobcat along?"

"I already invited her to play with us tomorrow, besides, I think I should really go to dinner at her house, she needs a best friend in town!"

Mrs. Koala seemed concerned. She said, "will Shawna Sheep, Joey Jaguar, and Zach Zebra be upset?"

"They will understand," Kimmie Koala said, then she ran back outside to where she left Becky Bobcat waiting. When she got to Becky Bobcat, she said, "I can come to dinner!"

The next day, Kimmie Koala woke up feeling thrilled about having the opportunity to introduce her new friend Becky Bobcat to all of her other friends. She was also curious to hear about the movie they saw the night before.

Kimmie Koala and Becky Bobcat met in the front yard and walked to the park together. When they arrived Shawna Sheep, Joey Jaguar, and Zach Zebra were already running around kicking the soccer ball among themselves.

Usually, they waited for everyone to show up before starting. Kimmie Koala's feelings were a little bit hurt when she noticed that her friends didn't wait for her.

"Hi, guys!" Kimmie Koala called to her friends.

They all looked over at her, smiled, and then kept passing the ball around. That's weird, Kimmie Koala thought, they're being kind of mean to me.

She tried again. "Hey guys, this is Becky Bobcat, she just moved here from the mountains!"

Becky Bobcat waved to the group.

"Hey Becky Bobcat," they all said in unison, but they never stopped their game.

Kimmie Koala noticed that Becky Bobcat's face looked sad. She wanted to help Becky Bobcat feel welcome, but her friends were ignoring her and she didn't know why.

"Don't worry about them, Becky Bobcat. They are probably just in the middle of a game. We can play our own game and wait until they're done." Kimmie Koala ran toward the playground and Becky Bobcat followed.

They raced to the top of the jungle gym and then down the slides, they played tag, they played hide and go seek, they played who can go highest on the swings, they played until they ran out of games to play.

"Now what should we do?" Becky Bobcat asked.

"Let's go play soccer now."

"But they still haven't finished their game."

Kimmie Koala shrugged. "Well, we gave them time to finish, let's just join in."

They walked back over to the field and Kimmie Koala said, "Okay, we are ready to play!"

"Well since you didn't come to the movies with us last night, we didn't think you were going to come play soccer today, so we only planned a game for three people," said Zach Zebra.

Kimmie Koala frowned, that really hurt her feelings. "That's not fair!" she said.

"It wasn't fair that you ditched us last night," said Shawna Sheep.

"I was having dinner with Becky Bobcat, she is new here and I was being nice. You can't be mad at me for that!"

"You could have at least let us know you weren't coming. We waited for you at the movie theater and almost missed the beginning," said Joey Jaguar.

"Or you could have invited your new friend to the movies," said Zach Zebra.

"I didn't know if she would want to meet so many new people all at once!"

Becky Bobcat chimed in, "I wouldn't have minded going to the movies. I didn't know you had plans when I invited you to dinner."

The friends started to play soccer again, leaving Kimmie Koala and Becky Bobcat on the sideline.

"I think I'm just going to go home," said Becky Bobcat, and she walked away from Kimmie Koala, to the exit of the park and all the way home.

Kimmie Koala waited at the park for a bit, hoping her friends would finally ask her to join in on the game, but when that didn't happen, she went home. She felt like she might cry, so she went straight to her bedroom when she got home.

Her mother knocked on the door and then popped her head inside. "Are you okay, sweetie?"

"All of my friends are mad at me!" Kimmie Koala started to cry now. "Shawna Sheep, Joey Jaguar, and Zach Zebra didn't let me play with them today because I didn't go to the movies with them. Becky Bobcat is mad at me because I didn't invite her to the movie and made my friends not like her. Now I have no friends!"

"There, there," Mrs. Koala whispered while she rubbed her daughter's back to calm her down. "Your friends will forgive you. You just need to learn that it's okay to have a lot of friends. While it's great to make new ones, you also can't forget about the old ones. They are both very very valuable. You can make new friends and keep the old. One is silver and the other is gold."

Kimmie Koala realized that she should have put herself in her friend's shoes and reached out to them. She shouldn't have just ditched them. She should have called them and explained the situation. She also realized that she could have invited her new friend to hang out with her other friends' sooner.

"I should say sorry to all of my friends, shouldn't I?" Kimmie Koala asked her mom.

"Yes, you should."

Kimmie Koala fell asleep with the plan to apologize to all of her friends in the morning. When the sun rose, so did Kimmie Koala. She went outside and saw Becky Bobcat next door.

"Hi, Becky Bobcat!" She called over and then walked to meet her. "I'm sorry about what happened yesterday. I should have checked with you about when you wanted to meet more new friends and I shouldn't have left my other friends out. I should have told you about the movies plans. I was just so excited that I didn't really think about how I would feel if it were me. I hope you will forgive me."

"Of course I can forgive you," said Becky Bobcat, "it was very nice of you to be my friend and want to introduce me to the others. You've been very kind, and besides, everyone makes mistakes!"

"I'm so glad!"

Kimmie Koala and Becky Bobcat then walked to the pool where all of the friends were that day. When they arrive they were all nice and welcoming this time. Kimmie Koala apologized for ditching them and they apologized for leaving her out and not being nicer. Kimmie Koala was happy to have old and new friends, and Becky Bobcat was happy to have all new friends. They all laughed and played games at the pool until the sun started to set and they had to run home for dinner.

Chapter Four

Rumors Hurt

THE END OF SUMMER was in sight and everyone was finishing up their summer homework assignments to turn in on the first day of school. The only exciting part was that Mr. Ostrich was going to be their teacher again because he got to move up a grade too.

Becky Bobcat was especially excited for school to start. She made some great friends during summer and knew that starting a new school would not be as scary as she thought. Her worries of having no one to eat lunch with or play with at recess had disappeared because she knew that she could sit with Shawna Sheep, Kimmie Koala, Joey Jaguar, and Zach Zebra.

On the very last day of summer vacation, Becky Bobcat was running to the park to meet her new friends for one last sunset session of hide and go seek. On her way to the park, she passed Frank Frog and Rachel Rat eating ice cream on the corner.

"Hi!" Becky Bobcat said as she came to a halt in front of them. "I'm Becky Bobcat and I'll be new in your class this year. I just moved here from the mountains."

"Are you going to eat us?" Rachel Rat asked.

"Thank you for offering!" Becky Bobcat stepped forward and tried to offer a handshake.

Frank Frog jumped in front of her paw and shouted, "Don't try to claw my friend's face open!"

Becky Bobcat was shocked that Frank Frog made up a lie, but before she could tell them she wasn't trying to claw anyone's face open, Rachel Rat and Frank Frog had run away. I hope they don't tell anyone I tried to claw Rachel Rat's face open, thought Becky Bobcat, because that's not true at all.

When she arrived at the park she saw her new friends there waiting for her on a park bench.

Shawna Sheep seemed timid when Becky Bobcat approached them. "Hi friends!" she called out.

They all waved.

Becky Bobcat, we just heard that you clawed at Rachel Rat's face. Is that true?" Joey Jaguar asked.

"No!" Becky Bobcat cried, "I was just trying to introduce myself and then Frank Frog started yelling that I was trying to hurt them!"

Everyone knew that Frank Frog and Rachel Rat were known for spreading rumors about their classmates, so they believed Becky Bobcat, unfortunately, not all of the other students did.

When Becky Bobcat arrived to class on her first day of school, everyone in the class looked scared. The seating chart had her in the front row next to Allen Anteater and Christina Cockroach. When she took her seat both classmates scooter farther away.

She saw Kimmie Koala in the row behind her and waved. Kimmie Koala smiled back, but didn't wave. When Zach Zebra walked into the classroom Becky Bobcat called out, "Hey Zach Zebra!"

"Hey," Zach Zebra mumbled, but he didn't even look at her.

Before Becky Bobcat had the chance to try to befriend anyone else in the class, Frank Frog and Rachel Rat walked in. The room got quiet because everyone was scared of them. They were the class bullies.

When they walked past Becky Bobcat's seat, Frank Frog shielded Rachel Rat, as if Becky Bobcat might attack them. It made her so mad that they spread the rumor about her that she had to say something.

"Why did you two lie about me?" Becky Bobcat raised her voice and stood up from her desk chair.

"Help! The bobcat is attacking me again! Help!" Rachel Rat shrieked and ran to the back of the classroom.

The entire class was staring with their eyes wide. They assumed it must be true that Becky Bobcat tried to claw Rachel Rat's face off and now she was trying again. The whole class started to tremble in terror and move away from Becky Bobcat, even Shawna Sheep, Kimmie Koala, Joey Jaguar, and Zach Zebra seemed to be afraid of her now.

"I'm not attacking her! I never attacked her! I'm just trying to make friends!" Becky Bobcat started to feel defensive. She didn't want her new classmates to think she was some kind of a monster.

Mr. Ostrich walked into the room just in time to see the whole thing happen. "Everyone calm down and take your seats please," he ordered.

The class obeyed and everyone returned to their seats in silence.

"We have a new student in class today, Becky Bobcat please stand up," Mr. Ostrich said. "Becky Bobcat moved here with her family over the summer and I expect that all of you will make her feel welcome here. Becky Bobcat, would you like to introduce yourself to the class?"

Becky Bobcat felt a huge lump in her throat. She was nervous to speak in front of a room full of peers who thought she was ferocious, but she knew she had to. In order to stop all the rumors and gossip about her, she needed to set it straight.

"I'm Becky Bobcat and I'm actually very nice. This summer I met Kimmie Koala because we are neighbors and we played together a lot. She introduced me to her friends and I spent a lot of time this summer playing games in the park and at the pool with them this summer. Everyone has been very nice to me, and I am very thankful. On the last day of summer, I tried to meet Frank Frog and Rachel Rat, but they were rude to me and they decided to tell you all that I attacked them, which isn't true. You can ask my friends Kimmie Koala, Shawna Sheep, Zach Zebra, and Joey Jaguar."

The class stared at Frank Frog and Rachel Rat. Their faces were red in embarrassment. Then the class stared at Kimmie Koala, Shawna Sheep, Zach Zebra, and Joey Jaguar. They were all smiling and clapping for their new friend. No one ever stood up to Frank Frog and Rachel Rat. The gossip they spread was always just assumed to be true.

"Well, well," said Mr. Ostrich, "looks like our first lesson of the year will be about spreading rumors and how it is hurtful to others. And this is a good time to remind you all of The Golden Rule. We should always treat others the way we would like to be treated. It's fairly simple, and I know that you are all very capable. Frank Frog and Rachel Rat, how would you like to be treated if you were new in town?"

"With kindness and respect," Rachel Rat said with her head down. Frank Frog nodded in agreement.

"That's how easy it is," said Mr. Ostrich, "just ask yourself how you would like to be treated."

Chapter Five

I Can Do It

"CLASS," MR. OSTRICH called out to get all of his student's attention. "We will be going on a field trip at the end of this month. I'm handing out permission slips now. Please turn them into me with a parent's signature by the end of the week."

He handed a stack of papers to the person in the front row of each line of desks and each student took one and passed the stack behind them.

"Cool!" Each student reacted with excitement when they saw what the field trip was.

The permission slip said: Dear Parents and Guardians, At the end of this month we will be taking a class trip to a rock climbing wall to practice our newly learned outdoor and teamwork skills. Sign and return this form to allow your child to attend and participate in this rock climbing adventure!

Shawna Sheep showed the form to her parents and said, "I'll climb to the top the fastest!"

Kimmie Koala showed the form to her parents and said, "Can I go on this field trip, please?!"

Joey Jaguar showed the form to his parents and said, "Isn't this awesome?"

Zach Zebra showed the form to his parents and said, "It's okay if you don't want me to go. It probably won't be very fun anyway."

Becky Bobcat showed the form to her parents and said, "It will be a fun way to spend time with my new friends and classmates!"

All of the students returned to form to Mr. Ostrich with a signature saying they could attend and participate in the rock climbing adventure.

When the day of the field trip came everyone came dressed ready to climb and their sneakers were tied tight. The air was filled with excitement. The students boarded the bus one by one and Mr. Ostrich was the last one on.

"Who is ready for a fun-filled afternoon?" he asked.

All of the students cheered loudly.

When they got to the rock climbing wall everyone unloaded from the bus and were greeted by an employee who told them all about the safety rules. Two people would climb at a time, but it wasn't a race. They were allowed to go as high up the wall as they wanted, and if they wanted to come down halfway that was okay. Also, if they climbed all the way to the top they could ring a bell.

"I'm going to climb all the way up as fast as I can and ring the bell!" Shawna Sheep called out.

Shawna Sheep was the first to get into a harness and step up to the wall. The end of a rope was hooked onto her harness and the employees at the rock climbing wall told her she was all set to start climbing. She made it look easy and scurried up the wall very quickly. Finally, she reached the top and rung the bell. The whole class cheered.

Other students took their turn; all being cheered on by the class. When it came time for Zach Zebra to climb up the wall, he realized that if he didn't make it up to ring the bell, he would be the first one to fail.

Zach Zebra was nervous. He had never climbed a rock wall before and he was afraid of heights. He knew that he could overcome his fear, but he was nervous that he might not have the strength and endurance to get him to the top of the wall.

When he stepped up to the wall and was hooked onto the end of the rope his palms started to sweat and his heart started to thump hard. He thought to himself, I can do this.

His class was standing behind him watching. If he didn't make it to the top and everyone else did, he was afraid that he would be laughed at.

"Go Zach Zebra!" the class was encouraging him just like they had for all of the participants before him.

"Alright Zach Zebra," said the employee, "you can start climbing when you're ready."

Zach Zebra grabbed a hold of the first plastic rock plastered onto the wall. He hoisted himself up so that he was standing on two other rocks. Okay, he thought, I'm on the wall, just keep climbing.

"You can do it Zach Zebra!" He could hear the class cheering.

He reached up for another rock on the wall and pulled himself up. He rested a foot on another rock to help hoist himself. The higher Zach Zebra got up the wall, the more tired he felt.

His arms and legs were getting sore and he was feeling a little out of breath. Zach Zebra looked up to see how much farther he had and then he looked down to see how far he had come. Unfortunately, he wasn't even halfway up the wall yet. He took a deep breath and reached out for another rock, but his other hand slipped and he fell off the wall.

The rope he was attached to caught him from falling to the ground, but now he was just hanging mid-air.

"You got this Zach Zebra!" His classmates were shouting.

"Are you okay?" the employee asked.

"Yes."

"Do you want to keep climbing or come down?"

Zach Zebra wanted to come down because he was afraid of failing, but he didn't want to give up just yet. "I want to keep climbing."

"Alright! Just grab back onto the wall and go ahead. Don't worry about falling, the rope will catch you," the employee called up to him.

Zach Zebra pulled himself back onto the wall but didn't know what his next move should be to climb higher up. The next rocks seemed to be too far away to reach.

'"I don't think I can do it!" he called down to his friends.

"Just try one more time!" Kimmie Koala called back.

"Don't give up!" Joey Jaguar shouted up to him.

"At least try to make it halfway!" Becky Bobcat suggested.

"We believe in you!" Shawna Sheep yelled up to encourage him.

The positive things his friends were saying to him made Zach Zebra get a second wind. He stretched his arm as far as he could and held tight to the next rock hold and jumped one foot up to a new spot. This burst of energy got him to the halfway point.

Zach Zebra was feeling tired again. He looked down and saw how far away he was from the ground. The sight made him start to feel scared. Zach Zebra already was afraid of heights and now on top of that fear he was exhausted!

I can do this, he told himself.

My friends believe in me, he told himself.

Don't give up, he told himself.

Mr. Ostrich, Shawna Sheep, Joey Jaguar, Kimmie Koala, Becky Bobcat, and the rest of the class was waiting on the ground for him to make a decision: climb higher or come back down.

Zach Zebra decided to give it one last try to get to the top and ring the bell. Two more big efforts and he was still just out of reach of the bell, but his arm muscles were so sore it felt like they were on fire.

"I'm ready to come down," Zach Zebra told the employee.

"Are you sure?" the employee asked, "you're almost there!"

Zach Zebra looked up at the bell and with one last burst of energy he leaped toward it and hit it with just the tip of his fingers. The whole class went wild clapping and hollering. It made Zach Zebra feel proud of himself.

He went in thinking he might not be able to even climb halfway up the wall and because he didn't give up he was able to prove himself wrong and ring that bell.

AFTERWORD

Thanks again for picking up this book! You are participating in making our world a better place.

For more of our Karma for Kids books please visit:
www.karmaforkidsbooks.wordpress.com
or
www.findyourwaypublishing.com

Find Norma MacDonald's books on Amazon.com.

The Many Adventures of Peppy the Emperor Penguin; Short Stories, Fuzzy Animals, and Life Lessons by Norma MacDonald

Ethan the Eagle and Friends; Short Stories, Fuzzy Animals, and Life Lessons by Norma MacDonald

Billy Brown Bear and Friends; Short Stories, Fuzzy Animals, and Life Lessons by Norma MacDonald

Humble Heron and Friends; Short Stories, Fuzzy Animals, and Life Lessons by Norma MacDonald

Peter Penguin and Friends; Short Stories, Fuzzy Animals, and Life Lessons by Norma MacDonald

Lucy Llama and Friends; Short Stories, Fuzzy Animals, and Life Lessons by Norma MacDonald

Other books that we recommend to help children learn important life lessons:

Guaranteed Success for Kindergarten; 50 Easy Things You Can Do Today! by Marrae Kimball

Guaranteed Success for Grade School; 50 Easy Things You Can Do Today! by Marrae Kimball

The Secret Combination to Middle School: Real Advice from Real Kids, Ideas for Success, and Much More! by Marrae Kimball

NORMA MACDONALD

If you have ideas for stories, please feel free to share and send them to:

Melissa Eshleman
Find Your Way Publishing, Inc.
PO Box 667
Norway, ME 04268
Melissa@findyourwaypublishing.com

www.findyourwaypublishing.com

Thank you!

Made in the USA
Las Vegas, NV
11 May 2022

48759083R00049